Diego and the Baby Sea Turtles

by Lisa Rao

illustrated by Warner McGee

Simon Spotlight/Nick Jr.
New York   London   Toronto   Sydney

Based on the TV series *Go, Diego, Go!*™ as seen on Nick Jr.®

SIMON SPOTLIGHT
An imprint of Simon & Schuster Children's Publishing Division
1230 Avenue of the Americas, New York, New York 10020
© 2008 Viacom International Inc. All rights reserved. NICK JR., *Go, Diego, Go!*, and
all related titles, logos, and characters are trademarks of Viacom International Inc.
All rights reserved, including the right of reproduction in whole or in part in any form.
SIMON SPOTLIGHT and colophon are registered trademarks of Simon & Schuster, Inc.
Manufactured in the United States of America
10 9
ISBN-13: 978-1-4169-5450-7
ISBN-10: 1-4169-5450-3
0710 LAK

¡Hola! I'm Diego. I'm an Animal Rescuer. It's nighttime, and I'm getting ready to head out to the beach for a special animal observation. I am going to need your help along the way! *¡A la aventura!* Let's go on an adventure!

Some baby animals are going to be born on the beach tonight! I'm going there to watch and make sure they reach the ocean safely.

The baby animals I'll be watching have a shell. Click the Camera is showing us pictures of four different baby animals. Do you see the one with a shell?

¡Sí! The baby sea turtle has a shell. Every year hundreds of baby sea turtles are born on beaches all over the world.

Alicia is on my Video Watc

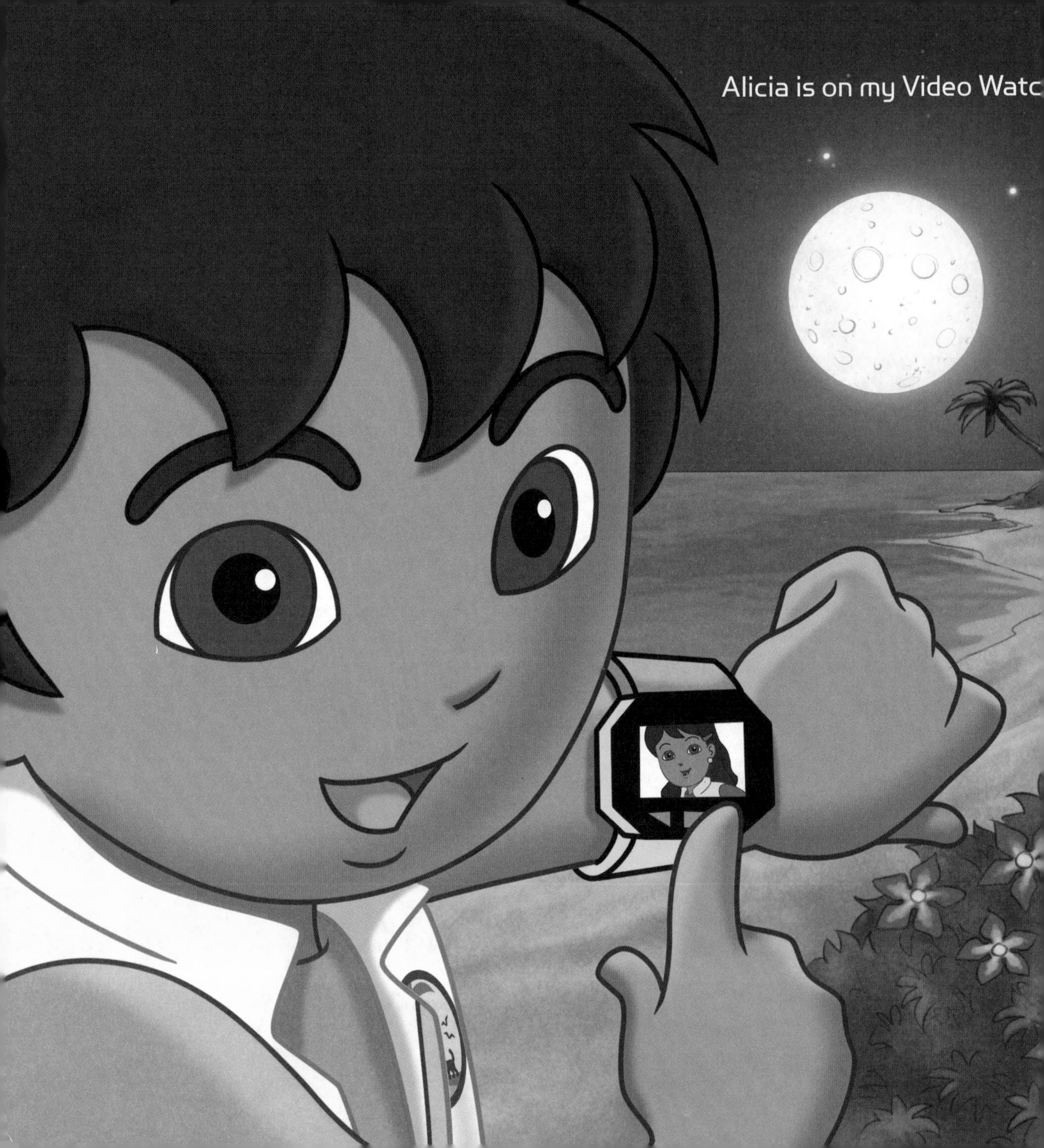

Alicia is telling me that a *mami* turtle digs a hole in the beach to bury her eggs. Then she covers the eggs with sand to protect them.

When the *mami* turtle is finished, she swims away. She is not there when her babies are born.

Alicia says that leatherback sea turtle eggs are the size of Ping-Pong balls!

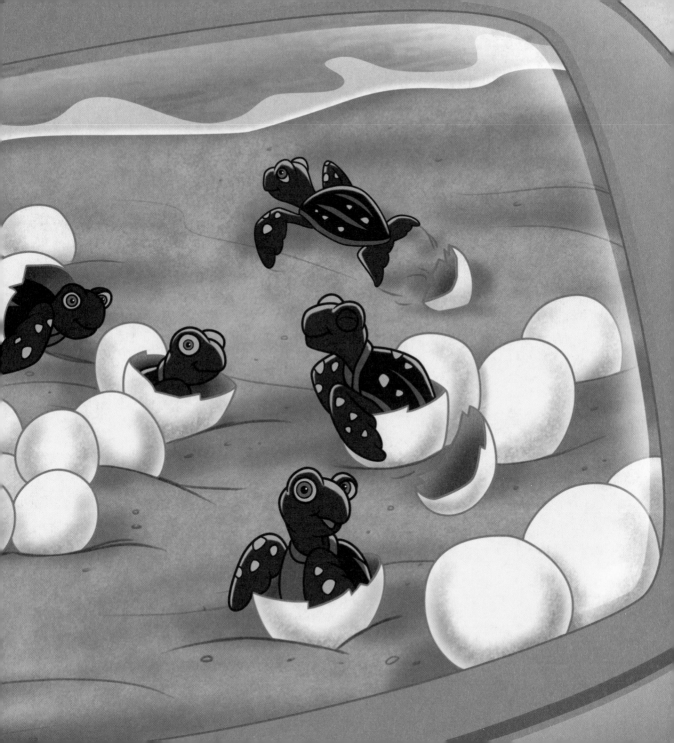

We need to get to Sea Turtle Beach, but look at all the garbage along the shore! We have to help clean up the beach so our sea creature friends can be safe. It's important to keep clear plastic bags out of the water. If sea creatures eat them, they can get sick.

Do you see another plastic bag on the beach? Point to it. I'll pick it up. Great pointing!

Now that we've cleaned up the garbage, we can go to Sea Turtle Beach. I'll
ok through my binoculars to make certain I can see the flags that Alicia and I
lanted on the beach a couple of months ago.

There are the flags! Sea turtles always return to the beach where they were born to lay their eggs. Every year sea turtles return to Sea Turtle Beach to lay their eggs, and Alicia and I plant flags to mark where the eggs are buried.

The beach cleanup took longer than I thought. How can I get to Sea Turtle Beach in time to see the turtles hatching? Maybe the dolphins can give me a ride. Thank you, dolphins! *¡Gracias!*

What a beautiful night! Soon the baby sea turtles will hatch from their eggs. Each flag shows where a pile of sea turtle eggs is buried.

How many flags do you see? Let's count them. *¡Una, dos, tres, cuatro, cinco, seis, siete, ocho, nueve, diez!* Wow! Ten piles of eggs. Each pile may have one hundred or more eggs. That will be a lot of baby sea turtles.

Look, the sand is starting to move! It's almost time for the baby sea turtles to appear! But wait—I see two bright lights at the end of the beach. If the baby turtles see those lights, they will get confused and crawl toward those lights instead of the moon! They won't make it into the ocean!

I need to find out what those two bright lights are. Rescue Pack can help.
He can transform into whatever I need. Say *"¡Actívate!"*
What can I use to get to the end of the beach fast?

A jet pack! Good thinking!

Oh, no! The Bobo Brothers are playing with flashlights. They need to turn those flashlights off so the baby turtles know which way to go. Freeze, Bobos!

That's better! Thanks for shutting off your flashlights, Bobos! We don't want to confuse the baby sea turtles. The only bright light we want them to see is the moonlight over the water, so that they will go toward the ocean.

Look! The baby sea turtles are hatching! *¡Fantástico!*

This one turtle is facing the wrong way. We can help it out. First let's turn it toward the water. Then let's put a red handkerchief over this flashlight so instead of a bright light, it will make a soft, red glow. Sea turtles like soft, red glows. The turtle will follow the flashlight right to the water!

Adiós, babies! Sea turtles always return to the beach where they were born to lay their eggs—no matter how far away they swim during their lifetime. So when they are grown, they will come to this beach to lay their own eggs!

That was a great animal adventure! I can't wait to record it in my Field Journal.

¡Gracias! Thanks for helping!

Did you know?

Do you know WEATHER it is a boy or girl?

Warm weather means baby girl sea turtles will hatch from the eggs. If the weather is cool, baby boy sea turtles will hatch.

"Ex-shell-ent" Swimmer

Adult leatherback sea turtles can swim really fast. They are faster swimmers than penguins.

Big Softies!

Leatherback sea turtles are the only turtles that do not have a hard shell. Their shell is covered with a thick, leathery skin. That's how they got their name!

Beaky Bites

Turtles do not have teeth. They use their sharp beaks to bite off leaves to eat.

Lots of Birthdays!

Leatherback sea turt may live for more tha one hundred years!